DISNEY'S

Mighty Joe Young

A novel by Hallie Marshall
Based on the motion picture from Walt Disney Pictures
Produced by Ted Hartley Tom Jacobson
Screenplay by Mark Rosenthal & Lawrence Konner
Directed by Ron Underwood

D1304486

DISNEY
PRESS

New York

First Edition
1 3 5 7 9 10 8 6 4 2

This book is set in 12-point Hiroshige Book.

Library of Congress Catalog Card Number: 97-80191
ISBN: 0-7868-4137-0 (paperback)

For more Disney Press fun, visit www.DisneyBooks.com

Chapter 1

Sunlight glazed the African mountains, tangled in the dense canopy of jungle, and sifted through to the forest floor. The air was filled with the sounds of insects and animal life, wild birds calling, and the smooth snap of a camera shutter.

Ruth Young zoomed in on the gorilla's expressive face. She took a picture, and another. The naturalist was half hidden in the undergrowth, and the gorilla was unconcerned. She was eating in a leisurely sort of way, stripping leaves from a branch. Her baby played nearby.

Ruth's daughter, Jill, was also playing. She crept to a tree close to the baby gorilla and peeked out at him. The baby saw her. He scampered to hide behind a different tree and looked out just as Jill had.

Jill ran to hide again. She sneaked another quick look. But the baby had moved, quicker than she, and was peering out to surprise her. From behind tree trunks, through the thick foliage, the two played peek-a-boo, until the gorilla noticed her absent offspring and let out a cry. The baby gave Jill a last, long look and scurried back to his mother.

Ruth whistled. It was her come-here-this-instant whistle, as Jill knew full well. She was in for it. "What did I tell you?" her mother asked. "It's not good for them to interact with us."

"But Joe started it!" Jill tried to defend herself.

"That wasn't Joe," Ruth told her daughter. "It was Marley." She put the camera back into its case and gathered up her field notes and equipment.

"No, it wasn't Marley," Jill insisted. "It was Joe."

"Joe is just a baby, Jill. He was too big to be Joe."

Jill shook her head. "Check," she said. "Check the pictures." Her voice held complete confidence.

As they headed back to camp, the sky above them went soft pink, then deepened with sunset colors. Ruth considered her daughter. The girl was smart and learning fast, and she was probably right.

Stars shone bright above the horizon. The Milky Way was a streak of white that dusted the dark peaks of the mountains. But in the jungle far below, there was a jangling noise, insistent and eerie, clanging like wind chimes made of tin cans. The noise was moving steadily, charging up the steep slopes.

Clang . . . clang . . . clang. A pack of mongrel dogs burst into a forest clearing. Tied around their necks were rawhide collars that bristled with scraps of raw metal. Behind the dogs, driving them onward, ran a half dozen African men with rifles. Ahead were a few others with *pangas*, mean-looking knives like machetes. The blades sliced silver through the night, slashing a pathway through the jungle.

Directing all this were two poachers, Garth and Strasser. Garth had a heavy Weatherby Mark V rifle slung across his back. He was a rough man and his instincts were sharp and cruel. When he came to a stick figure impaled in the earth, he yanked it from the ground and gave it over to Strasser.

Cigar clenched between his teeth, Strasser looked at it with contempt. The doll was three feet tall, crude, primitive, and grotesque. It was meant to serve as a warning. Strasser snapped the figure in two and tossed it into the underbrush. He shouldered his own rifle and ordered his men on. The hunting party swept forward, up the steep sides of the mountain.

The night breeze carried the ring of the dog collars into a peaceful valley. Camped there, within a circle of small huts, were Ruth Young and her daughter. The distant sound had not yet reached them. Ruth tucked Jill into bed. "What made you think the gorilla we saw today was Joe?"

"I was right," Jill said. "Wasn't I?"

Ruth nodded. "But my notes say that Joe is only six months old. Either I got confused, or he's a very unusual gorilla."

"I told you so." Jill's tone was singsong and smug.

"Yes, you did," Ruth told her. "And Mommy's going to write it down." She held up a dog-eared composition book, her field notes, and pointed to a page. "Right here. 'And then my trusted colleague, Dr. Jill Young, showed me the error of my ways.'"

Ruth leaned to kiss her daughter's cheek. "Now go to sleep," she said. Softly, she began a lullaby.

The lullaby was interrupted by the appearance of Kweli, the camp manager. When Jill smiled at him, he didn't smile back. "Kweli?" Ruth asked. "Kweli, what is it?"

"You should come," he said. "Quickly."

As soon as Ruth heard his words she was up. She grabbed the walking stick by the doorway and turned back to her daughter. "Stay here, Jill."

"But, Mommy—"

"Stay here," Ruth repeated. She followed Kweli out of the hut and joined a small gathering of Bahatu men. They were silent, unmoving, listening to the distant chiming of the dog collars. "Poachers," Ruth said. Her face was grim.

Kweli nodded in answer. In Swahili, Ruth said, "Let's go."

Standing just outside the hut, Jill watched her mother lead the men up the mountain trail. For a moment, Ruth was silhouetted by gentle moonlight. Then she was gone.

Chapter 2

Clang . . . clang . . . clang. Maddened with excitement, the dogs surged along through the woods, but the Africans were slowing, showing hesitancy. Garth heard them murmuring a few words over and over, *"N'gai Zamu . . . N'gai Zamu!"*

Garth tapped Strasser on the back. "Here they go again," he said.

Strasser called the men to a halt. "Forget your mystical nonsense," he growled. "There's only one thing you should be afraid of on this mountain. And it's looking you right in the face."

Not one of them could meet his eyes. Strasser stared them down. Then, turning abruptly, he knelt and picked something up from the ground. Strasser rubbed it between his fingers then deposited it into Garth's hand. "What is it?" Garth asked.

"Gorilla," Strasser said. "We're close."

Back in the camp, Jill could stand waiting no longer. She lifted a stainless-steel flashlight from a peg on the wall of the hut. She took off running after her mother.

The Africans fanned out. The dogs were barking, metal clappers clashing and ringing. As one, Strasser and Garth swung the rifles down, ejected and checked the clips, and rammed them home.

Just ahead, leaves shook, branches cracked, and trees trembled.

Black shapes scrambled and scattered and blurred into the darkness. The gorilla pack had sensed danger. They were trying to escape.

Eyes wide, Joe clung to his mother's back. There were flashes of brightness and explosions of sound, then his mother screamed and stumbled. Joe was flung aside, tumbling terrified into the high grass.

"Get the baby!" Garth was shouting.

Strasser lowered his rifle. "Don't shoot it!" he commanded. "They want the babies alive!"

Joe darted toward the still form of his mother. He cried out, desperate to reach her. But the two men cut him off and Joe fled.

"Over here!" Strasser yelled. "Bring the sack!"

Joe's anguish flared into fury. When Strasser drew close, Joe launched himself at the man, a small bundle of fur strengthened by frenzy.

Surprised, the poacher dropped his rifle and fell to the forest floor. He punched at the wild thing that had attacked him. As Strasser fumbled for the gun holstered at his side, Joe bit viciously down through the extended hand. Strasser howled in pain.

Garth leveled his rifle, aimed, and waited for a clear shot of the gorilla. First, Strasser was in the way, and then the figure of a woman seemingly came from nowhere. Ruth Young snatched the baby away from Strasser and ran with him toward the woods. Joe hung on for dear life.

Strasser clambered to his feet, one hand cradling the other. He tore the gun from his partner's grip and managed, somehow, to pull the trigger. Shots ripped through the night, but Ruth disappeared into the trees.

Panting, her heart pounding, Jill pelted up the mountain. Branches reached out to sting her and vines tripped her up, but she didn't stop.

Jill switched on her flashlight and waved the beam back and forth. Not far away another light answered. It was a known signal, familiar. With relief, Jill started toward it.

A form hurtled out of the underbrush and bowled her over. It was Joe, hugging her so tightly she could barely breathe. Jill gazed into his frightened eyes and felt a swift rush of terror. Gasping for air, she tried nevertheless to go totally silent and stay hidden.

His hand wrapped in a bloody rag, Strasser stalked into view. Garth followed, gun at the ready.

"She's got to be here somewhere," Strasser hissed. "She's got that devil with her."

Garth's voice was shaky, worried. "I think you may have hit the woman."

Coolly, Strasser responded, "So?"

With a shock, Jill realized they were speaking of her mother. She recoiled, but held on to Joe, willing him to be quiet.

Strasser contemplated his pain. "That little demon took off my trigger finger." In his own language he cursed, "*Monstrule!*"

"Your little monster couldn't have gone far," Garth assured him. "Want to keep looking, or . . .?"

"No," Strasser said. The rag he clutched was soaked with blood. His hand was throbbing. "Let's get out of here."

Footsteps cracked close to where Jill and Joe lay hidden, then faded away. Carefully, Jill sat up to see a light flash again in the distance. "Mom!" she whispered to the gorilla. "It's my mom."

At intervals, Jill replied with her own flashlight. She waited until her mother appeared, called in by the signal. "Shhhhh," Ruth cautioned.

"Mom, there were men . . . " Jill started, but then her mother staggered and collapsed beside her. "Mom?"

Blood was trickling out from the sleeve of Ruth's jacket. She covered it up, hiding it from Jill. As she did so, Joe whimpered. "Look who it is!" Ruth said, her words light, almost playful. "Hello, Joe."

"He's scared," Jill told her.

"Poor Joe. He lost his mother tonight." Ruth focused on her daughter. "He needs someone to protect him. Will you do that for me, Jill? Promise me you'll protect him. Promise me."

Jill was taken aback by her mother's behavior. She knew something was wrong. "I promise," she said. "I promise."

Her mother took Jill into her arms and rocked her as if she was a baby. Joe clung to them both, calming down, taking comfort from their warmth. Ruth began humming a soft lullaby . . . .

Chapter 3

Twelve years had passed since the death of Ruth Young, and her lullaby was still sung in Africa. It had become a hymn of sweetness and inspiration, a testament to courage and hope. Even Gregg O'Hara had heard it and had felt the strength behind the simple words. But Gregg wasn't thinking about any of that now—he was concentrating on the road.

Gregg drove like a man possessed, but his hands were steady on the wheel. He could possibly have been considered handsome were it not for the unkempt hair, dirty clothes, and five o'clock shadow.

As a village came into view and the road improved slightly, Gregg accelerated. The vehicle skidded into town and stopped just short of a man standing, unperturbed, right in the middle of the street.

Gregg jumped out and glanced around. "You must be Pindi," Gregg decided.

Pindi gave him a broad smile, slick and practiced. "The one and only, bro," he said.

Gregg examined Pindi's offerings professionally and critically. The assembled vehicles were battered and odd, adapted for the hunt. There was a flatbed lorry truck, and a couple of sport utility vehicles, one with a seat attached to the front hood. A group of surly-looking men lounged insolently nearby.

"Six men, three cars," Pindi pointed out. "Everything you asked for, Mr. O'Hara. And all paid for in advance, all out of Pindi's pocket."

Gregg held out a fat envelope. "I asked for experienced trackers," he said, a note of complaint in his voice.

Pindi snatched the envelope and rifled through the cash it contained. "These guys are the best in Africa," he assured Gregg. "The very best."

Gregg bent to stare straight into Pindi's face. The sunglasses hid the man's eyes, but Pindi stood unmoved and seemingly confident. Finally, Gregg went to his vehicle and flipped open the storage compartment in back.

The compartment revealed an impressive array of animal-tracking gadgetry. Pindi was impressed. As Gregg loaded a shining menace of a rifle, Pindi exclaimed, "Nice piece you got there. What are we hunting? Elephants?"

"We're not *hunting* anything," Gregg told him. "These are tranquilizer darts." He put the loaded rifle back into the compartment, then grabbed his binoculars. "Let's get started."

Pindi shrugged. "Ready when you are, boss. Just tell me where we're going."

Gregg panned the landscape through the binoculars. "There," he said. "Right there."

It was the highest mountain in the range, shrouded with cloud and mystery. Pindi glanced up and shuddered. "Uh, boss . . . we have a slight problem. No one goes there."

"We do," Gregg announced.

"We can't," Pindi stammered, "because of *N'gai Zamu*." Behind him, the other men fell silent, and Pindi began to whisper. "The legend of *N'gai Zamu* is something the locals here believe in. As the guardian of Mount Pangani, he returns every—"

"Every three generations," Gregg interrupted smoothly. "He comes back every three generations to protect his homeland."

Pindi's mouth dropped open in amazement. The story was ancient and sacred, so quietly passed on that it was virtually secret.

"You drive." Gregg dropped the keys to the vehicle into Pindi's hand. "You're not afraid of a legend, are you?"

Chapter 4

In a clearing high on the mountain, they parked the vehicles in a circle—an instinctive, defensive configuration. Gregg set up the equipment: three small audio dishes intended to triangulate and pinpoint sound, an infrared video camera on a tripod, and a large cage made of steel.

Pindi eyed the strange-looking pole Gregg lifted from the rear of the vehicle. "What's that, bro?"

"DNA plug gun," Gregg answered shortly. He slung a backpack over one shoulder. Inside was a set of headphones and a digital recorder. "We're ready," he said. "Let's go."

After they had settled into position, Gregg slipped the headphones over his ears. He listened for a while, his expression intent.

Pindi, impatiently, asked, "What are you listening to?"

"The jungle," Gregg said.

"The jungle, huh? I know a guy, he can get you a CD of jungle sounds really cheap. Even cheaper if you buy ten."

Gregg put up his hand. "Hey, Pindi? Feel free to shut up."

Pindi was about to add something indignant when Gregg stiffened. He was hearing something.

There was a *whoosh* and the clatter of a trap springing shut. Then the sound of an animal screeching. Gregg threw off the headphones and grabbed the DNA plug gun. Pindi followed him through the woods.

Several of Pindi's trackers were already surrounding the cage. Trapped inside, spitting and hissing, was a leopard. Pindi grinned. "How do you like that, boss? I told you these men were the best."

Gregg knelt to inspect the animal. "She's a beauty." Carefully, he extended the plug gun and pricked the leopard with it. She twitched and snarled, and a few of the men jumped back. "Okay," said Gregg. "Set her free."

Pindi gave him his finest and oiliest smile. "Why bring a cage if you are not collecting animals?"

"Blood samples, Pindi," Gregg replied. "I'm a zoologist, not a hunter."

"But I know a guy in Botswana, he'd pay you ten thousand American dollars for that leopard." Pindi was testing the waters.

Gregg wasn't interested. "He'd probably kill her and sell the skin."

"No, no, he's a collector," Pindi assured him.

"You can trust me, bro." He commanded his men to carry the trapped animal to the truck. But as they hefted the cage, Gregg stood in the way.

"Put the cat down," he said. "Now." There was something in his tone, the sudden stillness of his posture, which left no doubt. Gregg was not to be messed with. Neither was the leopard, which rendered a loud and furious cry.

As if in answer, a low rumble floated toward them like distant thunder. Gregg put on his headphones and tried to identify the noise. It was like nothing he'd heard before—a deep growling, then a rhythmic *pok-pok-pok-pok-pok*.

"*N'gai Zamu! N'gai Zamu!*" Pindi's men were frightened, and the East Indian, too. "Uh, excuse me," he said. "Time to flee, right?"

Something huge, something powerful and unseen was plowing a wake through the forest ahead. Whatever it was, it was coming right at them. The Africans broke and ran, with Pindi in the lead.

Gregg retreated, step by step, curious but undeniably spooked. He kept his eyes on the violent movement of the trees and listened to the crash of foliage. All around, birds lifted into the air, calling out high-pitched warnings.

There was a deafening howl. A gorilla, a giant gorilla, sprang into the clearing. The ground heaved and trembled. All the men, all the fancy equipment, and all the vehicles bounced into the air from the impact.

The gorilla's canines were fully exposed. His brown eyes were aglow as he let out another howl. Backlit by the sun, he seemed to encompass the forest. This gorilla stood, by any fast and frightened estimate, nearly fifteen feet tall.

The gorilla moved to the cage and peered inside. With a single hard slap, the gorilla smashed the cage, as if it were formed of matchsticks rather than metal. The leopard leaped out and dashed safely away. Rescue accomplished, the gorilla whirled and disappeared into the jungle.

Gregg stood staring, awestruck. He let out a breath, shook his head sharply, and ran over to his vehicle. "Come on!" he shouted. "We're going after him!"

"Who's this *we*?" Pindi asked. "Do you have a mouse in your pocket?"

"You saw it. I saw it." Gregg was out of his mind with excitement. "But nobody's ever going to believe it if I don't get pictures and a DNA sample. I'm not gonna spend the rest of my life as the nut who saw *N'gai Zamu* and couldn't prove it."

"I'm sorry for you," Pindi told him. "I am very sorry, but there is no way I'm chasing after that gorilla."

Gregg offered the best he could, the way into Pindi's heart. "I'll double your fee," he said. "I'll triple it. Come on."

Chapter 5

Counting the money in his head, figuring the exchange rate and the number of American dollars, Pindi called his people to order. Doors slammed shut, engines revved, and the men prepared for the chase. As one of the trackers loaded a rifle, it was snatched away. "Anyone shoots a live round out there, I shoot him," Gregg announced. "Understand?"

Before the man could respond, Gregg pressed a tranquilizer gun into his hands. "Use this only if you absolutely need to," Gregg said. He raised his voice to address the others, speaking in mostly Swahili: "When we catch up, I want you to herd him toward me. I have to be close to get a blood sample."

As the men nodded, Gregg inspected them gravely. He didn't trust them much, but they were all he had. "Okay," he said. "Let's go."

When the caravan of vehicles topped a hill in their pursuit, the giant gorilla was already racing to meet them. He roared and bared his teeth.

The man with the tranquilizer gun panicked and fired. The dart glanced off the animal's thick fur. Unhurt but enraged, the gorilla tackled the shooter's truck, sending it tumbling end over end into a ravine.

Gregg saw it happen from his vehicle. He was disgusted. "Where'd you find these idiots, Pindi?"

Pindi shrugged. Together, he and Gregg watched the gorilla spin around and head straight in their direction. The vehicle swerved crazily to avoid a collision. Just behind them, lurching in turn, was the truck with the hot seat attached to the hood. One of the trackers rode on the seat, readying a long chain with a clamp.

"No!" Gregg was yelling. "No, we don't want to . . . "

No one heard, or else no one was paying attention. The vehicle swung a hard right, and the man snapped the clamp around the gorilla's arm.

The chain unspooled rapidly, and when it drew taut the great ape had the advantage. Though the driver slammed on the brakes with both feet, the truck tilted upward, digging up clods of dirt, as the gorilla dragged the entire vehicle toward the forest.

Gregg and Pindi circled a stand of trees, trying to head the animal off. "Pull up right next to him," Gregg told Pindi. "I need to be close."

"Oh, sure," Pindi said. "You want me to hold him down for you, too?"

Gregg didn't answer. He was screwing a telescoping extension onto the DNA plug gun. Pindi glanced over. "I hope you are planning on *throwing* that at him, because . . . "

"Pindi!" Gregg shouted. "Look out!"

Strung tight between the gorilla and the hapless truck, the chain had become a trip wire. Pindi let go of the wheel and ducked. Gregg leaped out, hurdled the chain, and fell to the ground as the entire top was sheared off the vehicle. It careened to a broken stop.

The gorilla yanked hard at the chain and the attached truck jerked around. Then the chain, the winch, and the entire axle of the truck tore loose, and the animal was free.

He stood at the edge of the clearing, howling victory and beating his chest. Pindi and his men ran away in abject terror. The one vehicle available to them was the truck, and everyone piled in. Everyone but Gregg.

Gregg was hurt. He could barely stand up, but he was unlatching a case with a video camera. He hoisted the camera and staggered back toward the gorilla. Pindi stuck his head through the window of the truck. "Excuse me, boss," he called. "I would like to avoid being killed. Boss? Boss?"

Gregg didn't bother to acknowledge him. "Crazy Americans," Pindi said. He touched the driver on the arm. "Get us out of here."

Although the gorilla had once again disappeared, the path he had forged was easy to follow. Gregg stopped to listen. There was the sound of a twig breaking and a rustling of leaves.

The gorilla charged out from hiding and cuffed Gregg onto his back. The animal was in attack mode, teeth flashing, the hair on his crest erect. He grabbed Gregg by one foot and threw him into the air.

Helplessly, completely ineffectually, Gregg fought to defend himself as the gorilla mashed him up against a tree.

"Joe!" The voice came from thin air. "Joe! Stop!"

Dangling from the gorilla's hands, Gregg stared at the woman who had appeared in front of him. She was beautiful, clearly an angel. Clearly he was dead. "Oh, wow," Gregg said.

But no angel wore the kind of scowl that twisted this woman's face. She looked at Gregg as if he were the lowest form of life on earth. "Drop him, Joe," she ordered. So the gorilla did.

Gregg landed on his head and mercifully passed out.

Chapter 6

The cot was lumpy, narrow, and uncomfortable. Gregg attempted and failed to turn over. One of his arms was pinned into a sling, and he seemed to have acquired a turban. Cautiously, Gregg felt his head. It was swathed in bandages. He could hear people talking nearby, speaking in Swahili. "Where am I?" he asked them.

A man came to peer down at him. "You're lucky to be alive," he pronounced. "Allow me to introduce myself. My name is Kweli."

Gregg raised himself on one elbow. He winced. "I don't *feel* lucky."

"You crashed your vehicle," Kweli told him. "It is waiting for you outside."

"You're an injury behind," Gregg said. "The kicker was getting dropped on my head by *N'gai Zamu.*"

Kweli chuckled. "*N'gai Zamu* is just a legend, my friend."

"No, he's a giant gorilla with a mean backhand." Gregg struggled to sit up. "And there was a woman out in the jungle. She saved my life. A stunning, astoundingly beautiful . . . "

Kweli smiled. "You were dreaming, Mr. O'Hara."

Gregg started to shake his aching head, and then thought better of it. "I knew you were gonna say that."

"Stay here tonight, if you need to. After that, it would be better if you left." It wasn't a suggestion. Kweli's words constituted a command.

Squinting in the midday sun, Gregg walked gingerly out of the infirmary. He spotted his vehicle parked nearby, covered up with a tarp. Gregg limped over to inspect the damage.

It was an incomplete shadow of its former self. Gregg pulled back the tarp to discover his expensive equipment, a good deal of it broken, pitchforked into the back.

The video camera was there, muddy and dented, but seemingly in working condition. He popped open the tape compartment. It was empty. Gregg cursed, stringing together the worst words he knew in a variety of languages.

As he reloaded and tested the camera, a sweet sound drifted across the street. In front of the schoolhouse, some African children were singing. Leading them was the woman Gregg had mistaken for an angel.

The last notes of song lingered in the air and Jill Young smiled at her pupils. She clasped her hands together and spoke to them in Swahili, her voice warm with praise.

Gregg was seriously transfixed.

School over and the children dismissed, Jill slung her backpack over one shoulder. Kweli was waiting for her by the side of the road. She gave him a kiss on the cheek. "How's our guest?" she asked.

"Shaken up," Kweli answered. "Bruised. But awake."

"Good," Jill said. "Then he can leave."

Kweli smiled at her. "He's not a poacher, little one."

Jill grimaced. "That's what *he* says."

"His name is Gregory O'Hara. He's working for the California Animal Conservancy. My friends in Kimjayo tell me he is respected."

Jill looked at her oldest friend, her surrogate father. "He's an outsider, Kweli," she disagreed. "He can't be trusted."

"Listen to you," Kweli said. "Every day you're more like your mother."

"Why doesn't that seem like a compliment?" Jill asked, turning away. "I'm going to see if Joe's okay," she said. "I'll be back by nightfall."

At the edge of the village, a man was watching as

Jill started up a steep path. If Ruth Young had been suited for this place, Jill had been born to it. She strode along effortlessly, gracefully, making very little noise. It was all Gregg could do to keep up.

The rush of water amplified as Jill emerged from the woods. From her backpack, she took out a flashlight. Using the same motion her mother had used to summon her long ago, Jill waved the light back and forth.

Though it was daytime, the light cut through the deep green of the jungle, caught and flashed across tree trunks and foliage. Back and forth, here and there, Jill continued to signal.

And then Gregg heard it. Something crashing, something approaching, something coming toward them.

Chapter 7

The massive gorilla broke through the brush, cavorting rather like a puppy greeting his mistress. Jill ran her hands over him, making sure he was okay. "Hey, *rafki mkubwa*, how ya doing? Did those bad men scare you?"

Openmouthed, Gregg observed as the gorilla bowed his head so that Jill could scratch behind his ears. He was making a low, guttural vocalization, that sounded like a purr.

Satisfied that Joe was unhurt, Jill gave him a playful shove. She covered her face with her hands and started counting: "One . . . two . . . three . . . "

It took only seconds for the gorilla to respond. Head up, eyes wide, he scampered into the forest. Jill finished counting, " . . . eight . . . nine . . . ten! Ready or not, here I come!"

Anyone could have heard the great ape's passage, and anyone could see where he was hiding. He was so big, the tree he was using for cover barely obscured one leg.

Jill stomped around, pretending to seek him out. "Joe? Joe? Oh, I can't find Joe!" she exclaimed dramatically. "Oh, dear! Where could he be?"

Joe couldn't help peeking. "Come out, come out, wherever you are!" she called. And then, with a crow of discovery, of loud victory, she shouted, "I see you! I found you!"

Joe roared. She launched herself at him and gave him a tussle. Then, with a gleam of mischief in her eyes, she said, "Bye, Joe. Bye-bye!" She ran into the jungle, small enough to hide in it well.

Joe passed her by, circled her hiding place once or twice. Afraid he'd lost her, he began to whimper. He raised himself up on his hind legs and beat his chest in frustration. Before Jill could show herself, he started to rip up bushes, tearing them out by the roots.

And there was Gregg, exposed. "Nice monkey," he said soothingly. "No harm, no foul, big guy." Gregg held up his video camera. "It's a camera. See? Just a camera." The gorilla bared his teeth.

"Joe!" Jill had come out from hiding. "Joe! Get out of here, Joe! Run! Run, Joe! *Run! Run!*"

Joe seemed puzzled by her stern tone, but he didn't sense any real danger. As he turned and raced away, Jill rounded on Gregg. "We gotta stop meeting like this," he said sheepishly.

She snatched the camera from his grasp, ejected

the videotape, and smashed it against a tree. Gregg protested, "Hey! Hold on! That represents my life savings!"

Jill handed Gregg the mangled remains of the tape. She glared at him. "Next time I see you up here, I won't stop him. Understand?" She swung around and started back down the mountain.

Gregg followed her, talking, still cajoling. "Wait! Please? Tell me about Joe. That's his name, huh?" When she didn't respond, he switched to flattery, "Pretty incredible you've kept him hidden all these years. How'd you manage that?"

Her answer was short. "By keeping people like you off this mountain."

"Hey, you've got me all wrong," Gregg told her. "I don't wanna hurt the big fella, I just wanted to get some proof that he exists."

"What's the difference?" Jill spat out. "You go back and show them what you've found, and this mountain will be crawling with people."

Gregg sighed. "That'll happen anyway. This region is getting more and more unstable. It's gonna be tough to protect him."

"This is Joe's home, Mr. O'Hara." Jill was flushed with anger. "I either protect him or he dies. I don't have much choice."

"That's not true," Gregg said. "Listen. The place that sent me here, it's this place in California. They could take care of Joe. They have the facilities, and the budget—"

"A zoo!" Jill shivered. "You're talking about a zoo!"

"Not a zoo . . . a preserve," Gregg tried to reassure her. "He'd have a natural habitat, fixed up as much like his home as possible."

"Get off this mountain," Jill said. "Now."

Gregg looked at her. "I'll go, Miss Young. I'll go. And yes, I know who you are. I know who your mother was."

He smiled at Jill, rather sadly. "I've got a lot of respect for what you've done up here, and the last thing I wanna do is screw it up. But I found Joe, and, unfortunately, there were seven other guys with me."

Though Jill's face was averted, she was listening. "I'm telling you there's gonna be a major hunt starting tomorrow," Gregg informed her gently. "And I don't expect they'll give it up until one of them bags the prize. You should think about it."

He let her go then, watching as she fled sure-footed down the mountain. But she couldn't run from the truth in Gregg's words. Jill knew he was right.

Chapter 8

The grounds of the Raha Preserve in Botswana were extensive and lush. A few giraffes browsed on the topmost branches of trees within sight of an opulent house. Mr. Anderson, a buttoned-down zoo director, watched them through the windows. With a smile, he turned and said, "Quite an impressive facility you have here, Mr. Strasser."

Strasser nodded and settled comfortably into a leather chair. Anderson went on. "Why is it that you keep such a low profile about this wonderful place?"

"Our only interest," Strasser said smoothly, "is the well-being of our animals."

Anderson placed some photos on the table in front of Strasser. They showed a full-grown tiger in a small enclosure. "You can see how depressed Morris is," Anderson said. "He's grown out of his habitat, and our zoo doesn't have the budget to do anything about it. That's why he needs a new home."

Jill and Joe hide from Strasser in the brush.

An animal large enough to make such a footprint is supposed to exist only in legends.

"Drop him, Joe," Jill orders.

Joe roars in anger as the clamp tightens around his arm.

Jill signals for Joe to
come to her.

Jill gives Joe a hug.

Gregg hides in the forest, snapping photos of the incredible gorilla.

Joe sits forlornly in the truck, confused and unhappy about leaving the jungle.

Jill is the only one who can calm Joe when he arrives at the conservancy.

Even though familiar trees and flowers surround him, Joe feels trapped in his new habitat.

Joe crashes the fund-raising party, intent on finding Strasser, his tormentor.

Loose in the urban jungle of Hollywood, Joe searches for an escape.

Joe races to the rescue of a boy in danger on the broken Ferris wheel.

Strasser picked up a picture to examine it more closely. On one hand he wore a black glovelike apparatus with a manufactured thumb and forefinger. "Poor thing," Strasser said. "Yes, he will be much happier here on our preserve. Back to the wild. Free again."

A door opened behind the two men, and Garth put his head in to announce, "Phone for you, *Mister* Strasser. It's urgent."

Strasser rose. "Will you excuse me, Mr. Anderson?" Smoothly, he left the one room and entered another, a secret place that would have given the well-meaning Anderson nightmares.

A man in a white smock was packing rhinoceros horns into boxes labeled as medicinal supplies bound for China. On the wall behind him was a chart that listed various animal species, and their respective prices.

Strasser gave the photo of Morris to Garth. "See what our friends in China will give us for a Bengal tiger."

"Looks like a big fella!" Garth was excited. "We could set a new record!" He gestured toward the phone. "Over there."

Strasser picked up the receiver. "Strasser," he said.

"It's about time already!" The voice was indistinct, crackling long-distance. "You know how long

I am waiting for you? A man can only put in so much change—"

"What do you want, Pindi?" Strasser was irritated. He took up a rhino horn and idly turned it over in his hands.

Pindi was standing at a pay phone, too public for what he wanted to say. He spoke furtively, "It's not what *I* want, boss. It's what *you* want. How about a giant gorilla?"

"Talk," Strasser barked.

"A gorilla as big as three men. Two thousand pounds at least."

"You've been drinking," Strasser accused. "Haven't you?"

"Swear to God, boss," Pindi maintained. "Saw him with my own two eyes."

"Don't waste my time again," Strasser growled. He slammed the phone down into its cradle.

On his end, Pindi heard the click of disconnection, then a dial tone. "I'll catch him," Pindi said into the void. "I'll catch him and charge you double, *madar chode*."

The children were waiting patiently in front of the village schoolhouse. Their teacher was a little late. Jill was standing stock-still in the middle of the street, staring at two trucks that had pulled up in front of the gas station. A third vehicle joined them.

Pindi had arrived with a new group of men, all armed to the teeth.

It was Kweli who let the girls into the school. As they filed in, Jill pointed to the trucks. "When did they show up?"

"Daybreak," he said. "This is just the beginning. More will come."

Jill's expression took on determination. "We'll stop them."

"How will we?" he asked. "Every year, this area grows more populated. All the other gorillas have moved to safer lands, but Joe has stayed behind."

"The other gorillas rejected Joe because of his size," Jill claimed. "That's why he's still here."

"Maybe," Kweli said, "or maybe it's because he's too attached to you."

"I promised. I promised my mother I would protect Joe."

Kweli bowed his head. He understood both the strength of her oath and the impossibility of fulfilling it.

"I promised," Jill repeated. She turned away from Kweli and caught sight of Gregg, who was packing his belongings into his battered vehicle. She observed Gregg for a while, considering the situation. Then she crossed over to speak to him. "Leaving?" she asked.

He nodded. "I'm gonna head up the mountain.

See if I can't throw some of the poachers off his trail. I'm not just gonna sit on my hands. It's my fault these guys are here."

"They would have come anyway. And they'll keep on coming." There was a pause. Then, matter-of-factly, she said, "If we're going to do this, I'd have to go with him."

"What?" Gregg was confused. "Who?"

"I've been thinking about it." Jill held Gregg's eyes with her own. "It seems like the place you were talking about is the best chance Joe's got."

"You're serious, aren't you?" He leaned against the vehicle to think things over. "Okay," he decided. "Let me make some calls."

"There's one condition," Jill warned him.

"Name it."

"I'm in charge of Joe."

Gregg shrugged. "No problem."

"Promise me," she said. "You've got to promise."

He gazed at Jill, and he saw the fear within her decision. Everything in her life, and in Joe's life, was about to change. "Jill, I *swear* to you. You'll be in charge. Okay?"

"Okay." She tried very hard to smile.

Chapter 9

Jill ran flat-out and fluid, as if she were the wild and innocent child she had once been. Joe chased behind her, enjoying the game, unaware that this was maybe the last chance they had to play in the mountains where they had grown up together.

To Jill, the landscape had never seemed more beautiful. "I don't know what to do," she said aloud to Joe. She stroked his dark face, worry etched on her own. "I just don't know what else to do."

The sky was blue and the day inviting at the wildlife conservancy in California. A warm wind rustled through the trees, and a flock of blackbirds lifted and wheeled above a singing waterfall. But there was also a railing, tall fencing, carefully disguised enclosures, and a moat to define the boundaries of a human-made habitat, all encircled by a sprawling campus of stucco buildings.

Dr. Harry Ruben, chief zoologist and the director of the conservancy, was walking alongside Dr.

Cecily Banks, a veterinarian with long braids stuffed under a baseball cap. "You know this is crazy," Harry told her. "We send the guy to get a leopard, and he finds a giant gorilla."

"Don't even pretend to be upset," Cecily said. "You'll be famous."

"You know how much it cost to convert the tiger habitat?" he complained. "Try half our operating budget."

Cecily grinned. "You'll be on the cover of *National Geographic*."

He returned the smile. "Hey, I just said it was crazy. I didn't say it wasn't worth it."

As the car with Gregg and Jill approached the gate, a worker in a conservancy uniform waved them through. And when the livestock truck followed, the worker picked up his walkie-talkie. "Main gate to Dr. Banks. They're pulling up now."

Cecily Banks got the message. She clicked off her walkie-talkie and turned to yell to everyone in earshot. "Elvis is in the building," she shouted. "I repeat. Elvis is in the building."

On her order, workers in matching uniforms started to move into their positions. A crane lowered a platform to straddle the moat. The moat was there to define the habitat that was to be Joe's new home.

Then came a ruckus. From all around, the other animals were making their various noises.

Screeching, snarling, howling, bellowing, the air was filled with sound. "They smell him," Cecily told Harry Ruben.

"Who?" Harry asked. "Gregg or the gorilla?"

Cecily shot the director a look of caution as Gregg emerged from the car. "I'm confused, O'Hara," Harry said. "I thought you were bringing back a giant gorilla."

Gregg nodded in greeting. "Hey, Harry."

"But security tells me you've requested no fire hoses, no tranquilizer guns, no restraints of any kind."

Gregg said, "I'd like you to meet—"

"How are we supposed to control the animal?" Harry interrupted. "What do we need? A rolled-up newspaper?" His voice trailed off as Jill got out of the car. Quietly, she shut the door behind her.

"Jill Young, this is Dr. Harry Ruben, the director of our conservancy." Gregg performed the introductions. "And this is Dr. Cecily Banks, our chief veterinarian."

Jill shook their hands politely. "I want you both to know how much I appreciate your making these special arrangements."

"Our pleasure," Cecily said.

"You're welcome." Harry responded automatically, continuing to struggle with his reservations.

"So," Gregg said, "whaddya say we show Joe his new home?"

Chapter 10

From inside the livestock truck, Joe was growling. Jack and Vern, two graduate-school conservancy workers, could hear him. The low sound wasn't exactly hair-raising, but it was threatening nonetheless. "Easy, big boy," Jack said. "Easy now."

Vern offered something else, "Don't forget who's gonna feed you."

As they raised the gate to the back of the trailer, Jill came up behind them. "Thanks, guys," she said. "I'll take it from here."

The two were happy to comply. Jill took out a flashlight, one she'd brought with her from Africa. She turned it on and waved the beam back and forth, exactly as she had done in the jungle.

Because the light was in front of Jill, Joe could see only her silhouette. Shaken by the long journey and unfamiliar surroundings, Joe kept up his growling complaint.

The entire conservancy staff listened with concern. Harry took a step back, and another. Only Gregg stood his ground. "You sure she knows what she's doing?" Harry whispered into his ear.

"Just watch," Gregg said.

Jill continued to wave the flashlight and the trailer began to rock. Heavy footsteps pounded the floorboards. "Come on, Joe," Jill coaxed softly in a soothing tone. "Come on."

Reluctantly, the massive gorilla emerged. Absolute astonishment greeted the staff's first sight of Joe. Gregg grinned at their slack-jawed reactions.

Cecily nudged Harry. "That is one mighty big, huge gorilla," she said.

At the sound of her voice, Joe turned. He glared at the assembled crowd. There were too many people surrounding him, more humans than he'd ever seen. He spun around and scampered back into the safety of the trailer.

"Now what?" Harry complained.

Jill walked to the doorway. "Come on, ya big baby. There's nothing to be scared of." She went into the trailer and sat beside him.

Joe hunkered down, making himself as small as possible for an oversized great ape. He produced a number of sounds, a pattern of pants and hoots that gorillas use to communicate. To the conservancy staff, it almost seemed as if Joe was trying to reason with Jill.

"Well," said Harry. "That was amusing and pointless." He nodded toward Jack and Vern, who had been prepped in advance. The two started to mash sedatives into a bowl of food meant for Joe.

The trailer had started to shake, to rock back and forth, jostled by a large and upset gorilla. Jill leaped out and approached the men. "If you just give me a few minutes, I'm sure I can get him to calm down." Then she saw the bowl of food. "What are they doing?"

"What we should have done from the beginning," Harry told her. "We're sedating him."

"No," Jill said. "You are not!" She faced Jack and Vern. "You two, *you* stop."

"Hello?" the director called them to order. "Who pays your salaries?" To Jill, Harry said, "I'm told you and Joe have a special connection. But I happen to run this conservancy, and Jack and Vern will do as I say."

Jill whirled to face Gregg. "You said I'd be in charge of Joe. You promised me. You lied."

Before Gregg could say anything, Harry filled Jill in. "It's a simple cause-and-effect relationship. I'm in charge here. When I tell my people to sedate an animal, they do it. And we're sedating this gorilla."

Jill was distraught and still angry as Gregg unlocked the door to her new apartment in the main building. "You said I was going to be in charge of Joe. I should be sleeping down there with him, not staying in this . . . this . . . this *cage*."

The apartment was a modest one-bedroom unit

with a TV, bed, couch, and kitchenette. "Hey," Gregg said, "this place isn't bad."

Feeling claustrophobic, Jill went to the window to get some air. The top was solid, double-paned glass. The bottom cranked open a scant three inches. "What's wrong with this window? That's all it opens? That's all?"

Jill was panicking and hyperventilating. "This is wrong," she gasped. "This is all wrong. Please fix it . . . please do something . . . . "

Gregg snatched up a pillow and set it against the top portion of the window. He gave it one hard blow, shattering the glass. Methodically, he removed the remaining shards and threw them away, dusted off the pillow, and put it back carefully on the couch where he had found it.

Jill stared at him, speechless. He looked into her eyes. "I'll do *everything* I can for you. Anything."

In a small voice, she said, "Thank you."

Except for the occasional call of an animal, the conservancy complex was quiet at night. With the effects of the sedatives mostly worn off, Joe slumped beneath a grouping of newly planted saplings. The fence that ringed the moat in his habitat was electrified. Near the gate was the transformer. The metal box produced an unfamiliar and menacing buzz, a constant disturbing hum.

Chapter 11

The Cadillac drew to a stop in front of the conservancy's main building, and a distinguished-looking man in a suit emerged. Elliot Baker was the chairman of the board, and Harry was intimidated by him. "Hello, Elliot," he said. "Good to see you again."

Elliot nodded to acknowledge Harry and Cecily Banks. Then he rubbed his hands together. "So? Let's go see your new acquisition."

Cecily said, "Right this way." She led the two men toward Joe's habitat.

Harry was talking, trying to garner some glory for himself. "I always had a suspicion that the legend of *N'gai Zamu* might have some truth to it," he told the chairman. "It was just a hunch, a gut feeling, but I sent my field zoologist out to the Pangani forest to check it out."

Cecily couldn't believe what she was hearing. "That field zoologist, *Dr. Gregg O'Hara*, had a theory, and Joe's blood work confirms it," she

44

announced firmly. "The gorillas in the Pangani Mountains carry a recessive gene that pops up every four or five generations with a rare form of giantism."

"So that's where the legend comes from!" Elliot Baker was impressed. "That zoologist of yours—what's his name again?"

Begrudgingly, Harry told him, "Gregg O'Hara."

"Pretty sharp." Elliot gave Gregg his due as Cecily smiled.

When they arrived at the observation railing that surrounded Joe's habitat, the gorilla was nowhere to be seen. Elliot asked, "Where is he?"

In imitation of Jill, Harry tried to call him. "Joe? Joe, come!" With an apologetic look at Elliot, he said, "I told him the chairman of the board was coming by, and Joe *promised* to say hello."

"Well, I don't see him." The chairman was disappointed.

"We'll find him," Harry vowed. "We'll feed him. Cecily, open the gate."

Hesitantly, Cecily selected the key to the security gate. She regarded the director with a measure of doubt. "Harry? Are you sure?"

Jill was going over the requirements for Joe's diet with Jack. The meeting was interrupted by an urgent summons from Cecily's walkie-talkie. Jill got up and raced toward Joe's habitat. Gregg had heard the message, too, and he was right behind her.

Inside the enclosure, several conservancy workers were hastily loading heavy-duty tranquilizer rifles. The gorilla was snarling and beating his chest, performing a classic threat display, which was scaring Harry to the core. The director was hiding in the midst of a clump of foliage, hands shaking, white as a sheet.

As the men trained their weapons on Joe, Jill and Gregg burst into the line of fire. "Stop!" Gregg yelled. "Just stop!"

Later on, Cecily cornered Gregg. "I was wondering why you hadn't taken off yet. Normally, you're out the door as soon as an animal's settled in his habitat."

Gregg asked her, "What are you saying?"

"I think Mr. World Traveler has goo-goo eyes for the gorilla girl." Cecily grinned at him.

"I think you've got an active imagination," Gregg said, though it was clear she had hit a nerve. And he needed to do something about it.

When he knocked at Jill's door that afternoon, she opened it right away, almost as if she'd been expecting him. Gregg waited there uncomfortably, simply looking in. "I like what you've done with the place."

The TV was gone, the mattress was on the floor,

and potted ferns had been placed here and there to form a personal jungle. "It's better," Jill said. "Too bad it's always so cold." She smiled. "Somebody broke my window."

Jill motioned for him to come in. But Gregg stood rooted beside the doorway. "Listen," she said, "I know why you're here, and before you say anything, I owe you an apology."

"Jill, that's not why—"

"The other day, when I accused you of lying to me, I got carried away. I realize you gave me the best promise you could."

"Forget about it." Gregg had something more important to tell her. "I just came by to say that Joe looks real good out there—"

"I know it," Jill interrupted. "This is working out better than I could ever have expected."

"—and that I'm hitting the road," Gregg concluded.

"Where are you going?" she asked.

"Back to Africa . . . for a couple of months."

"No kidding?" Jill tried to keep things light. "When do you leave?"

The reply was one word. "Now."

When Jill just nodded, Gregg struggled on, attempting nonchalance. "It's the job, you know. Always on the road. It's what I like anyway. I can't stand to be caged up."

Her eyes strayed to the walls of her tiny apartment, to the open-air window. Jill knew what he meant.

"You and Joe will be okay," Gregg said.

"Of course we will. We'll see you when you get back."

Gregg turned to leave. "I'll call you."

Chapter 12

"The remarkable size of this gorilla made him a natural target for poachers. Fortunately, the California Animal Conservancy . . . " Strasser's attention was riveted on the television. The program continued with pictorial shots of Joe, both in Africa and in his new habitat.

"My God," Strasser exclaimed. "Pindi was right." He shook his head in disbelief, eyes alight with greed. "He's the most beautiful animal I have ever seen."

"And the most valuable," Garth added. "That's for sure."

"I want him," Strasser said. "He belongs here with me."

Garth thought it over. "It'll be a bit tricky, won't it? They're not gonna want to part with—"

"Wait!" Strasser ordered. "Be quiet." Intercut with the televised pictures of Joe were photographs of Jill and her mother.

" . . . was raised from infancy by Jill Young, the

daughter of famed primatologist Ruth Young. Their closeness stems from a tragic bond. Joe's mother and Jill's mother were both killed by poachers twelve years ago, in the Pangani Forest, orphaning them together on the same night."

Strasser's expression changed from desire to fierce hatred. "Bloody hell," he cursed. "That's the *monstrule*, the little monster that . . . " Garth glanced at Strasser's hand: tanned, manicured, and maimed.

Strasser flexed his remaining fingers and strapped on the leather prosthetic. "I am always amazed how—if you wait long enough—the opportunity for justice finally comes. Book us two tickets to America. We're going to pay a visit to this 'remarkable' animal."

Harry led a group of VIPs around the grounds. They were all well-heeled and capable of making major contributions to the conservancy. Within the group of listeners, looking almost respectable, was Garth. His suit was expensive, his shoes handmade, and his violent nature hidden.

Next to Garth, an impatient man interrupted Harry's speech. "Excuse me," he interjected, "now can we see Joe?"

Harry turned on the charm. "You certainly *can* see Joe . . . for the mere price of a Diamond Circle

Benefactor Ticket to our upcoming benefit." The VIPs laughed at this and Garth took the moment to slip away from the others unnoticed.

The tour was over and Harry was waving good-bye to his VIPs when Cecily and Jill drove up in an electric cart. Jill wore a conservancy T-shirt and she'd been working hard all day. "Harry, that's all we have left of the lobelia leaves for Joe. Did you by any chance place that new order?"

"Of course, I—" Harry broke off, looking guilty. "Actually, perhaps, I . . . "

"I wouldn't be surprised if you forgot, considering you have *so* much on your mind." Jill began. But the lobelia leaves were forgotten with the sudden appearance of Gregg.

He was dressed in his safari outfit, smiling at her. "When did you get back?" she asked, surprised.

"Today." When Jill didn't say anything, he pretended his feelings were hurt. "Hey," he said. "Don't act so excited."

The two walked away, trying to break the tension. "What time do they let you off for the day?" Gregg wanted to know.

"Anytime I want."

"When'd you start running the place?" Gregg was bantering, yet he was still impressed. "Look.

I'm hungry. Let me take you to dinner. I know a nice place, a good restaurant. Okay?"

Garth strode toward Joe's habitat fast, but not fast enough to attract attention. He moved to the edge of the moat and scanned the area for Joe. The big gorilla was behind some saplings, moving slowly, browsing.

Garth removed something from his pocket. It was a dog collar, festooned with scraps of tin and a few rusty keys. Garth looked around quickly, then shook the collar. *Clang . . . clang . . . clang!*

Joe reacted immediately to the sound, deeply imprinted as a danger signal in his mind. He rose up and growled, then howled and pounded his chest. He charged at Garth, heedlessly throwing himself against the electrified fence that bordered his habitat. Joe roared at the shock and recoiled.

Garth smiled. "You remember. Don't you?"

Chapter 13

"So, *this* is what you call a nice meal in a good restaurant?" Jill inquired of Gregg. She sneaked another french fry from the container of fish and chips they were sharing. Several people had built bonfires along the shoreline of Venice Beach, and the night was warm and magical.

"Yeah," he answered, grinning at Jill.

"Don't point that smile at me," she cautioned him. "I'm still mad at you for taking off and leaving me here all alone."

Gregg said, "I'm sorry. I had things to do. And, besides, you weren't alone. You had Joe."

"That's right," Jill's voice was quiet. "Me and Joe. Just like always."

"Growing up with him around . . . what's it been like for you?" he asked. "I mean, most guys are afraid of girls' *fathers*. I can just see some guy telling *Joe* that he'd have you home by midnight."

"I never had anyone to bring me home anyway." Jill shrugged. "All that stuff, I don't even know what it's like."

"All what stuff?"

Jill turned away from him, defensive, dismissive. "Whatever you want to call it. That love stuff. Being in love."

"Well," he began, "it's kinda like getting bit by a Makiki spider."

She gave him a sharp glance. "Oh, yeah? How's that?"

Gregg touched her forehead. "You'll get a kind of a fever . . . "

"A fever?" she asked. "How high?"

"Pretty high."

"Interesting," Jill said. "Hallucinations with that?"

"Oh, yeah," Gregg told her. "And you'll . . . uh . . . find yourself saying things. Lots of things." They were face-to-face. Gregg wanted badly to kiss her. And it seemed as though she was thinking of letting him.

But it didn't happen. Jill's beeper intervened. A message scrolled across that read: JOE TROUBLE.

Joe was on a major rampage, destroying everything within reach. A small army of workers from the conservancy was trying to stem the flow of water from a broken irrigation pipe. "Half of our water system is gone!" Vern told Jill when she arrived at a run, gasping for breath. Vern was covered in mud.

"He's ripping out saplings one after another,"

Jack explained. "The roots are tangled in the piping . . . one good yank, and on comes the flood."

"You ever see Joe act like this before?" Gregg asked Jill.

"No," she said. "Never." She watched Joe hurl a tree across the moat.

"Do you have any idea of what might be causing this?" Gregg asked.

Jill didn't. And it scared her. "I wish I did."

The next morning, Jill went for a talk with Elliot Baker, Mr. Chairman of the Board. "We have to postpone the benefit," she informed him.

"What? Why?"

"I know it's late notice," she said, "but there's something wrong with Joe. He shouldn't be exposed to a bunch of strangers."

"I heard he calmed down today." Elliot shot back a snow-white cuff to expose his watch. "Do you really think it's necessary to—"

"We need to postpone the benefit," Jill persisted.

The chairman gave her a piercing look. "Miss Young, let me give you some advice. Stop worrying about Joe, and start thinking about what you'll wear tomorrow night. It had better be something pretty."

Head down, fuming and frustrated, Jill stormed out

of the chairman's office. She bumped into a man walking toward her from the opposite direction. "Oh, excuse me," she apologized.

The man righted himself and smiled at Jill politely. "No. Pardon me," he said with an accent she couldn't quite place. "It was my fault entirely." Then he gave a start and gazed into her face.

Flustered, Jill drew back, but he continued to stare. "I'm so sorry," he said. "It's just that you look . . . it's just . . . you must be Jill Young."

"Yes, I am."

"You look . . . like her." The man went on to explain, "I'm Andre Strasser, a good friend of your mother's. I knew her when she was only a little older than you are now, and you were a tiny thing. What an incredible woman she was."

With his damaged hand concealed in his pocket and a pleasant smile, Strasser came across as a friendly conservationist.

Jill bought it. "How wonderful to meet you. What are you doing here?"

"I've come to talk to your chairman, Mr. Elliot Baker." Strasser pretended to be slightly uncomfortable. "You see, I am here for Joe. And, in a way, for your mother, too."

His words rising in make-believe passion, Strasser went on. "I believe your mother would

56

agree with me. She would agree that a magnificent animal like Joe needs more space—like on the Raha Preserve I run in Botswana."

The mention of her mother, and the memory of her own promise, hit hard at Jill's sense of responsibility. "Raha?" she asked. "A preserve?"

"I have twenty thousand acres where animals are free to roam. I would like to offer this freedom to Joe." Strasser sighed. "It is such a shame to see Joe *imprisoned* in a human-made habitat . . . and being *used* as an attraction to raise money."

Strasser shook his head sadly at the inhumanity of it all. His ploy was working. Jill was absolutely crestfallen.

"Oh, dear, I've upset you." Strasser's tone oozed comfort. "I only mean to offer an alternative. I will be attending the event tomorrow night. Perhaps we can talk more about this matter then."

"I'll look forward to it," she said.

Strasser knew he had her. It was time to take his leave. "Now, I must be going. I have business to attend to. If you're ever in Botswana . . . " He handed Jill his card, cream-colored and elegant. "Good day, Miss Young."

Chapter 14

A large tent had been set up near Joe's habitat in preparation for the benefit. One side was flush against the railing that surrounded his moat. The canvas provided a curtain between Joe and the VIP guests. At the proper moment, Harry planned to reveal the gorilla with a flourish—like someone unveiling a grand new piece of statuary.

Inside the tent, a tasteful party was in progress. An assemblage of fifty VIPs, all dressed to the nines, mingled with members of the staff. Tables had been arranged in a semicircle around the podium from which Elliot Baker and Harry would lecture, do a little show-and-tell, and convince the guests to contribute to the conservancy.

Cecily and Gregg passed through the gathering, seeking out Harry. The director was ill at ease in a tuxedo, rehearsing his part of the speech.

"Harry," Gregg said. "It's a party. Try to relax."

And then Jill came into the tent. She was stunning, ravishing, drop-dead gorgeous. All heads swiveled in her direction. Jill blushed and faltered near the entryway. For a second, it seemed as though she was about to turn tail and run away.

Cecily poked Gregg in the back. "I picked out the dress," she said. "Aren't I smart?"

"Brilliant." It was the only word he could manage. Gregg picked up a glass of champagne for Jill and headed toward her.

From across the room, two pairs of eyes had observed Jill's entrance and the follow-up. Neither man missed much, ever. It was the hunting instinct, finely honed. "Quite a turnout they have here." Garth pointed out the obvious.

"All the better," Strasser said.

When Elliot Baker tapped on the microphone, begging for the crowd's attention, Strasser put down his drink. "Let's go," he told Garth. Together, the men moved unobtrusively toward the exit.

Well-practiced in the art of public speaking, Elliot proceeded smoothly. "When was the last time you laid eyes on something so unique, so spectacular, that it literally took your breath away? Well, prepare yourselves, for tonight you will have such an experience."

Just outside the tent, Strasser and Garth exchanged glances. They had heard the chairman's words, and they thoroughly agreed. If things went according to *their* plans, those attending the benefit were in for the "experience" of a lifetime.

Garth slipped his hand into his jacket and withdrew the dog collar. He showed it to Strasser and grinned. "Shhhh," Strasser said. He indicated a pair of men negotiating the sidewalk unsteadily, weaving along and talking.

Jack and Vern had had a bit much to drink, but Jack didn't really think so. "There's nothing in that punch," he slurred. "I could drink twelve more glasses and not feel a thing."

Smack! Jack collided with Garth. Garth dropped the dog collar, and Vern stooped to retrieve it. Picking it up by one of the rusty keys that served as a clapper against the tin, Vern peered at the collar. "So sorry," he said. "Here's your . . . uh . . . key chain."

Garth snatched the collar away from Vern, and Strasser thanked them both coolly. Vern and Jack stumbled on, neither one the wiser.

Joe was feeding on lobelia leaves when something tugged at his attention. A slight clattering, a jangling, a timpani of chimes—*clang . . . clang . . . clang.* Faint at first, the sound was growing louder.

Joe raised his head to listen, the hair on his neck bristling. He moved toward the source of the noise, toward the moat, toward the tent full of people.

Garth stood safely at the railing on the other side

of the moat. He rattled the dog collar again. Joe answered with a growl. Then Strasser stepped into the light, and his cold eyes locked with those of the gorilla.

Joe went berserk. He howled and bared his teeth.

"So you haven't forgotten me?" Strasser smiled nastily. "Good." He displayed his mangled hand. "Have you forgotten this?"

Garth rattled the collar over and over, enjoying the effect. Joe charged at the men and was stopped by the moat, and the electric fence that surrounded it.

"What do you think the big guy is worth?" Garth asked. "A couple of million?"

"After we sell him off piece by piece, who knows how much he'll bring," Strasser speculated.

"Hang the collar there," Strasser instructed Garth. "Hang it where he can see it. We'll come back for it after . . . "

Garth hung the dog collar on the fence. It jangled lightly in the breeze. "Come now," Strasser said. "We've done our job here."

Joe was in a truly frightening state, driven by memory into outrage. He paced this way and that, shaking his head, until he focused, finally, on a tall tree in his habitat. He pounded his chest and howled.

Chapter 15

At the podium, Elliot Baker was winding down his portion of the presentation. "To talk about our remarkable new acquisition, I'd like to ask the director of our conservancy to come up . . ."

A roar from outside the tent drowned out Baker's voice. The audience jumped in their seats, startled. The chairman kept his composure, however, and made a joke of the interruption: "I suppose there's no need to add to *that* introduction. And now, to tell you more about Joe, is Dr. Harry Ruben."

Harry was suffering from stage fright. Cecily gave him a discreet push to the microphone. He began to speak: "In the time it took you to drive here tonight, three species disappeared from Earth. Never to return."

Pok-pok-pok-pok. Beyond the thin barrier of the curtain, Joe could be heard beating his chest and growling. Jill looked at Gregg with concern. His face mirrored her mounting anxiety.

The director raised his voice to be heard above

the disturbance outside. "Here at the conservancy, we say this is a tragedy." Another spine-tingling roar from Joe punctuated Harry's words. "Obviously, Joe agrees."

The audience laughed at the joke. They were twittering with excitement, not knowing enough to be afraid. Jill glanced around and caught the eye of Strasser.

He had returned, along with Garth, and was sitting in place at his table. Strasser gave Jill a sympathetic nod, indicating that he was also worried about the gorilla's aggressive behavior.

Unnerved by the noises coming from behind the curtain, Harry read the rest of his speech directly from his notes. "Tonight, rather than focusing on what we've lost, I'm going to introduce you to something we've found."

There was a tremendous crash and a cracking sound outside. Harry paged through to the conclusion: "Ladies and gentlemen, the California Animal Conservancy proudly presents our newest member, Mighty Joe—"

Before Harry could say "Young," a tall tree came crashing through the curtain. By using the tree as a bridge, the gorilla had figured out how to span the electric fence and the moat. Chest heaving, Joe stood on the platform where the podium had been, before the tree had smashed it into splinters.

His entrance was greeted with mostly silence, and a few nervous giggles. Some of the guests clearly thought this was all part of the show. But Jill knew better. She approached him carefully. "Joe? Hey, Joe? I'm right here. You hear me? Take it easy, Joe. We don't want to scare anybody."

Joe was listening, his head bowed, and was beginning to calm down, until he spotted Strasser. Strasser stared directly at the gorilla, provoking him, challenging him into action.

With a roar, Joe went after his enemy, knocking tables and chairs aside. One table struck Jill and sent her sprawling against the wall. She sank to the floor.

Inside the tent was pandemonium. Joe plowed through the party, swatting people out of his way. He grabbed a man and hoisted him into the air. It wasn't Strasser. Angrily, Joe flung the man away.

Gregg had reached Jill where she lay. She was unhurt but stunned, watching Joe in disbelief. "My God," Jill said. "What's wrong with him?"

"We've got to bring him down," Gregg told her. "I'm going for the tranquilizer guns."

"No! Let me try . . . " Her words went unheard. Gregg was already gone.

Jill hurled herself against the streaming, screaming tide of fleeing people. She was trying to get to Joe. She pushed past Elliot Baker, just as a security guard with a tranquilizer rifle raised his gun and fired. The dart missed Joe completely, but it hit Baker. The chairman crumpled to the ground.

Aware of the danger, atypically frightened, Strasser scrambled toward the exit—and Joe chased him. When a guest fell in the gorilla's path, Joe heedlessly stepped on his leg, crushing it. The man shouted in agony.

At last, Joe had Strasser trapped against the wall. The gorilla threw a table out of the way, and was reaching for his enemy when there came an explosion from a rifle. Joe dropped to all fours, revealing Gregg. Gregg lowered his tranquilizer gun, a pained expression on his face.

But one tranquilizer dart wasn't enough to stop Mighty Joe. Other conservancy workers peppered the gorilla with a hail of darts. Joe swiped at the stinging things, stumbled backward, and fell heavily to the floor.

Then Jill was at his side, stroking the black fur, crying. Gregg looked sorry. In fact, he looked sick.

A grim-faced reporter turned to the camera. In the background, the torn tent sagged. It was totally destroyed. *"Officials are saying they don't know what caused the rampage here tonight . . . standing with me is the chairman of the conservancy, Mr. Elliot Baker . . ."*

"Mr. Baker, what is the conservancy doing to assure the public that Joe won't attack again?"

"Joe has been transferred to a special concrete bunker, which is reinforced by steel bars. He won't be able to attack anyone, or to escape."

"What about after you let him out?"

"That won't be happening anytime soon," Elliot assured the media. "In the meantime, we will do anything, *anything* necessary to ensure the safety of the public."

Chapter 16

Rifle at the ready, an animal-control officer had been posted by the bunker that was now the gorilla's new home. The holding room had one narrow window crisscrossed by steel bars.

Joe was drugged and despondent. Though he was crouched over, his head nearly touched the ceiling. Outside the bunker, Jill and Gregg hovered like distraught parents. "Joe? Joe, look at me," Jill pleaded. "Over here, big guy."

She tried to touch him through the bars, but Joe didn't respond. "I *knew* something was wrong with him. I tried to get Elliot to postpone . . . "

"What do you think happened out there?" Gregg asked.

Jill shook her head. "Joe would never have hurt all those people without provocation. Something must have got to him."

"Something," Gregg said. "Or someone."

The idea hadn't yet occurred to Jill. She thought for a while, considering it. And then Harry came up beside her. "Jill?" he said. "Can I talk to you for a minute?"

With a last worried look at Joe, Jill followed Harry out. This left Gregg alone with the gorilla for the first time since Joe had dropped the zoologist on his head.

Gregg leaned against the bars. "This wasn't in the brochure, was it? I promised you wouldn't be put in a cage. I'm sorry, Joe," he apologized. "I'm really sorry. I helped to put you here. And now I'm going to do everything I can to get you out."

Gregg reached through to stroke Joe's massive forearm. Gently, Joe curled his fingers around Gregg's hand.

Harry led Jill to the observation area. "The City Attorney talked to Baker," he informed her. "It wasn't my decision, and there's nothing I can do about it."

"About what?" she asked.

"Joe stays in there until they decide what to do with him."

"In *there*? Harry, look at him!" Jill cried. "He's depressed, he won't eat. If he stays in there, he'll die within days."

"So, sue me." Harry shrugged. "Everyone else is."

"Harry! Either you tell them you're getting Joe out of there, or I will!"

"Don't you *get it*?" Harry's voice rose in desperation. "This is way beyond you and me. Joe freaked out on some very influential people. He's a public relations nightmare. No zoo will take on a two-thousand-pound killer gorilla."

"Joe is not a killer!" Jill was adamant.

"And unless you can write a check for a few million dollars to buy him a very big backyard somewhere, Joe's got no place to go."

"That's it?" Jill was incredulous. "That's all? You're not going to do anything?"

Harry had nothing more to say. He could see he'd lost her friendship and her respect, and it bothered him—actually shamed him. The director turned and left the room, brushing shoulders with Gregg on the way. Judging from the expression on Gregg's face, he had overheard the whole thing.

"I need your help," Jill told Gregg.

"You got it," he said.

Arrangements were made, plans formed, and a plane reserved and waiting. When Jill, Gregg, and Cecily approached the officer guarding the bunker, he came forward to meet them. "Good evening," Cecily said. She gave him her sweetest smile.

When he smiled back, Cecily and Jill breezed on past him. "Hey!" the officer challenged them. "Hey! Wait a minute!"

"We're conservancy doctors," Gregg said. "Your job is to stay here and guard the door." Though puzzled, the officer took up his position at the doorway, rifle at his side.

Cecily brought out a key and unlocked Joe's cage. "Come on, Joe," Jill called. "We're leaving. Let's get you out of here."

The prospect of freedom had a stronger effect on Joe than the heavy sedatives in his system. He clambered to his feet and emerged from his prison.

"What the hell are you people doing?" The animal-control officer had followed them in and now held his rifle steady on Joe.

Cecily introduced herself. "I'm Dr. Cecily Banks, the head veterinarian here. I'm taking Joe in for a CAT scan."

"I take my orders from Mr. Elliot Baker," the officer maintained. "Until I hear otherwise, the gorilla goes back in the holding tank. Now."

Suddenly, the officer grabbed at his neck. Jill had fired the tranquilizer rifle. The guard crumpled to the ground.

Cecily went outside and blinked a flashlight into the night. In answer, a tractor-trailer backed up toward the building. "Okay," Cecily called quietly. "Bring him out."

Once the gorilla was safely inside the trailer, a man emerged from the truck. It was Strasser. "Jill, the plane is on the runway now," he said. "We must hurry."

It was time to say good-bye. Cecily told Joe, "I'm going to miss your ugly face. You be good."

"And don't start a fight with anyone bigger than you." Another voice chimed in. Harry stepped out from the shadows. He shuffled a little with embarrassment, and then he said, "You'd better leave through the west gate. The guard there got called away on important business."

Jill gave him a hug. "You're not such a coward after all."

When she didn't let up, Harry grinned. "Okay, you can let me go now."

"Write to me when you get settled." It was Cecily's turn for a hug.

"I promise," Jill said, and then she turned to Gregg. They looked into each other's eyes. "You coming to the airport?" Jill asked him.

"No," he said. His voice was strained. "I'll stay here and keep people away from that bunker. Give you a good head start before they realize he's gone."

Jill stammered, "Well, if you're ever in Botswana, you can take me out to a nice meal in a good restaurant. As long as you're not afraid to tell Joe that you'll have me home by mid—"

Gregg kissed her, a real kiss, the kiss he'd been wanting to give her from the first time he'd thought she was an angel. He released her finally, and spoke to the dark form in the trailer. "Take care of her for me. Will you?"

"Jill!" Strasser's whisper was urgent. "We must go!"

Jill hopped into the truck, and Strasser climbed in behind her. Garth was at the wheel. She was sandwiched between the two men. "Don't worry, Jill," Strasser said. "Soon Joe will be back home again."

Chapter 17

"How many minutes do you give it before the whole world knows Joe's missing?" Cecily asked.

"Five," Gregg answered. "How many minutes do you give it before we're both looking through the want ads?"

She smiled. "Six."

Just then, Jack and Vern drove up in a conservancy vehicle. "Hey," Gregg called, "what are you guys doing here so late?"

"Baker wants the tent cleaned up as soon as possible," Jack said.

Vern reached into the vehicle and took out a cardboard box. "Check out the loot we plundered in the wake of mass party panic! This is some weird lost and found." To demonstrate, he displayed a high-heeled shoe and a toupee.

"Somebody's head is *cold*!" Jack said. "And we've got the fun job of getting this stuff back to everybody."

Digging around in the box again, Vern pulled out

the jangling dog collar. Gregg grabbed for it. "Where did you find this?" he asked.

"Oh, that was by the habitat," Vern said. He looked at Jack. "Guess we'll have to find those two guys again."

"*What two guys?*" Gregg was beginning to get the picture.

"Vern, you remember those two," Jack said. "What do you think that one guy was—Russian or maybe Lithuanian?"

Gregg snatched the keys from Jack's hand and sprinted to the vehicle. By then, Cecily had an inkling of what was going on. "Gregg!" she shouted after him. "Be careful!"

It was a rough ride. Garth was driving fast. The tractor-trailer lurched and bumped, and Jill heard a *thud* from the back of the trailer. "Please," she begged, "be careful."

"Always worrying, eh?" Strasser asked. "Your mother was a worrier, too. Worrying about the gorillas. It made her a lot of enemies. It led to a terrible tragedy."

"My mother was brave," Jill insisted.

"So are you, my dear." In the slashes of light from the streetlamps they passed, Strasser had taken on a sinister sheen. For the first time, Jill noticed his strange leather hand. Strasser caught the direction of her glance. "It's not so pretty, I know."

She looked away. "I'm sorry. What happened?"

"You could say I had an encounter with a monster," Strasser said. "A little *monstrule*."

The foreign word struck a chord deep within Jill's memory. She saw herself hiding, holding on to a young Joe. She remembered the poachers, their voices in the darkness. She remembered, and she knew.

Unsure of her next move, Jill glanced around the cab of the truck, trying to figure out some means of escape, some weapon to use to free herself. She caught sight of a conservancy vehicle in the side-view mirror, coming up fast behind them. Somehow, she knew it was Gregg.

Jill stiffened, and Strasser felt it. He saw the vehicle, too. The lies he had told, the stories he had relayed, and the deception he had constructed were over.

Adrenaline pumping through her, Jill lost it. "Murderer!" she screamed. She slammed her elbow into Strasser's nose and his hands reflexively covered his face. It was time for Garth. Jill grabbed his hair and smacked his head against the dashboard.

The truck swerved wildly and Jill kicked and clawed her way over Strasser to get to the passenger door. She opened it and clutched onto the side-view mirror. Jill swung out, but the truck was going too fast for her to safely drop down.

From the truck, Gregg saw her. Jill was dangling, swinging, crashing again and again against Strasser's truck. And then she fell, hitting the running board, bouncing hard onto the asphalt. Two cars narrowly missed her.

In the trailer, Joe was going crazy. He had seen Jill in trouble through the slats, and he was trying to get to her. The trailer lurched back and forth, the truck swayed in turn, and Jill raised up to yell futilely, her words lost in the rush of distance. "Joe!" she cried. "Get out! Joe!"

Strasser looked back at the crumpled form on the roadway. Jill was alive, moving, shouting something. "Drive," he ordered. Garth floored it.

It was Gregg who got to Jill first, scooping her up and saving her. She was bloody and bruised, but she didn't seem to notice. "What have I done?" Jill was saying. "Oh, God. Oh, Mother. What have I done?"

She asked Gregg, "Do you know who they are?"

"Yes, I know." Gregg carried her to the Blazer. "Come on," he said. "Let's go get him back."

Chapter 18

It was a picture-postcard night on Hollywood Boulevard. Lots of neon, tourists, hasslers, and hustlers. Then a tractor-trailer broke into the scene, weaving, tires screeching, rocking with the frenzied motion of the gorilla in the back.

The truck jackknifed, skidded, and slid to a stop, the trailer at an acute angle to the cab. From the sidewalks, out of the stores and restaurants and theaters, came people.

A loud growl stopped them all cold. A huge fist punched through the top of the trailer. The crowd surged backward as Joe fought to emerge, pulling himself out and onto the trailer's roof.

The gorilla encountered such a confusion of upturned faces that he missed seeing Strasser and Garth, neither of them hurt, both climbing from the wreckage of the truck. "We better go," Garth hissed. "Police'll be here any minute."

Strasser didn't care. He wasn't listening. He reached into the truck and took out his hunting cap and a leather case. He put the cap on his head, and melted into the darkness. Automatically, Garth followed his lead. Strasser the poacher was back.

Joe dropped down from the trailer. Flashbulbs glittered across his dark fur. "Hey! It's that gorilla that was on TV!" People were taking photographs, then running away.

In a four-point stance, Joe moved down the street. It was an urban jungle, made up of concrete and steel, artificial lights, and human beings.

He bumped against a Mercedes and the alarm went off immediately. Joe wheeled and hammered at the car until it went silent. But the tumult continued—blaring horns, sirens, and shouting.

Within the crowd there was a kid, street-tough but young. When his eyes met those of the gorilla, the boy's face took on a look of wonder. "Hey, Joe!"

The kid pointed the way for the gorilla to escape, away from the noise, away from the gathering of vehicles and police cars. Joe watched the boy closely, then turned and went in the direction the boy had told him to go.

From the doorway of Mann's Chinese Theater, patrons watched the gorilla approach. A ticket-taker went numb with fright as the massive face of Joe appeared close to her glass booth, curiously peering in.

"Up there!" someone was yelling. It was an

LAPD policeman. The giant gorilla was scaling the theater, climbing high into the Hollywood sky. From the roof, Joe could see hills and trees in the distance, things that were vaguely familiar.

The police had their rifles ready, loaded, and aimed to fire, but the gorilla had already disappeared over the top of the theater.

Gregg pulled the truck to a stop near the wreckage of the tractor-trailer. Joe was nowhere to be seen. "He couldn't have gotten far," Gregg said.

Jill was overwhelmed with fear and frustration. She climbed atop the truck and shouted, "Joe! Joe! Come, Joe!"

Over her cries, people were yelling, "Over here! This way!" They gestured toward Mann's, toward the clutch of emergency vehicles, toward the place where Joe had last been sighted.

As Jill and Gregg ran toward the theater, the police were regrouping and a helicopter swept into the air. One officer was talking into a radio: "Orders are shoot to kill," he said. "The gorilla is extremely dangerous."

"No! He's not dangerous!" Jill had overheard. "He's not dangerous! You're dangerous! You all are!"

"She didn't mean that." Gregg pulled her away. The policeman was gazing at Jill as if she were two seconds away from arrest. Gregg told her, "Better cool it."

"They're going to shoot him!" Jill was frantic.

"Not if we find him first." He observed the helicopter heading toward the hills. He took Jill by the arm. "Let's follow them. Come on."

Together, they raced back toward the truck. They didn't know it, but the vehicle had been staked out. Strasser smiled as Gregg and Jill got in and took off. It was as if something made sense to him that Garth couldn't figure out. "What are you doing?" Garth asked.

Strasser opened the case he had retrieved from the truck. Efficiently, he assembled the rifle inside. "What are you doing?" Garth repeated. "You don't think we can *still* get the gorilla, do you?"

Strasser didn't bother to answer. "We need a car," he said. "Now."

The world-famous white *Hollywood* sign stood on the hillside. A shadow passed across it, and a large gorilla passed through an *O*. Joe paused and looked around.

In the distance, a beam of light swept across the sky. It was a searchlight, the one for the Palisades Ocean Amusement Park, placed as a beacon to attract customers. But to Joe, it looked like a flashlight signal. And that meant a summons from Jill.

Chapter 19

A guy had pulled over to join the gawkers and watch the activity on Hollywood Boulevard. When the rifle poked in through his open window and pressed up against his cheek, the driver didn't even flinch. He sighed with resignation. "Fifth time this year."

He took his soda from the cup holder and the garage-door opener off the dashboard. Clearly, the man had been through this all before. Garth hauled him out of the car. "Hey! I was going!" the man whined. "No need to be so pushy about it."

Strasser and Garth jumped into the stolen vehicle and drove away, fast into the night.

There was a constant flow of noise, a sound like the rush of a river. A stream of passing lights split the hills around Hollywood. The congestion of the L.A. Freeway confused Joe, but he knew he had to cross it. He could see the beacon not far away, beckoning him to Jill.

As Joe stepped into the first few lanes, cars scattered, screeched, and skidded around him. But miraculously, none crashed. Almost ceremoniously, the oncoming traffic came to a halt as Joe lumbered across.

The gorilla climbed over the center divider, and the same thing happened in the southbound lane. Nobody had an accident. No one honked or screamed. The highway was quiet. Los Angeles was in awe.

"Any idea where he might've headed?" Gregg was driving, still following the helicopters and swarm of police.

Suddenly something snagged her attention. Shining over the horizon, shifting here and there across the sky, was a searchlight. "There. That's where he'll go," she said. "He'll think that's me calling him."

Gregg nodded and accelerated. As he did so, another car discreetly came along from behind. It was Garth and Strasser. On the trail.

At the Palisades Ocean Park the searchlight rotated amongst a festival of lights—illuminated booths, the midway, arcades, rides. The Ferris wheel was a neon blur spinning grandly above it all.

A young couple stopped to kiss underneath the

arched neon gateway to the park. A growl interrupted the exchange. The two parted, stumbling away in fright, and Joe appeared beneath the arch.

The panic came in slow motion. It took a while for the gorilla's entrance to make a difference in the busy amusement park.

A line of kids waited patiently to ride on the Ferris wheel. One of them, Jason, was talking with his mother: "Mom, I don't think I can let you go with me this time."

"Why not?" she asked him.

"Because the last time, after you ate two hot dogs, you threw up," he said. "Remember?"

"What if I promise to throw up over the side?" She smiled at her son, and he giggled at her joke.

"But, Mom," he persisted. "I think I should do this ride by myself."

His mother was reluctant, but then she gave in. "Okay," she said. "I'll watch you." Above them the wheel turned slowly, majestically, the occupants waving as they topped and came over the crest.

Joe had found the searchlight, but there was no sign of Jill. He paid very little attention to the humans around him. They were scrambling and screaming, clearing his way.

Jill and Gregg had at last arrived and were fighting against the crush of people fleeing the park.

"He's gotta be here," Jill gasped. "Do you see him?"

Gregg was looking around, seeking the main source of the commotion. "Over there," he said. "Let's go."

Strasser was using the scope of his rifle as a viewfinder. Hunter's cap firmly in place, he was scanning the place and the people.

Garth knocked the rifle away. "Hold on, now," he said. "Just who are you aiming at?"

His partner's eyes were deadly. "If that girl starts telling people who we really are, our whole cover operation will be blown."

Garth was horrified. "She's not an animal. That's a human being you're about to kill."

Strasser raised the rifle again, aligned the sights, aimed for the target. Just in time, Garth slapped the gun from his hands.

Blam! Strasser's shot, altered by Garth, hit a klieg light near Jill and Gregg. The light exploded, glass shattered, and Gregg hit the ground, pulling Jill along with him.

Sparks showered from the broken light, igniting the sawdust and straw that amusement parks use to fill in potholes, soak up mud, and buffer the floors of many rides.

It took only a second or two, before a small flame spread toward a pool of oil at the base of the

Ferris wheel. The flame danced over the oil and engulfed several sacks of sawdust. They smoldered then erupted into a much larger fire.

The Ferris wheel operator abandoned the controls to spray the flames with an extinguisher. The wheel kept turning unchecked, and still the fire grew.

Strasser fixed his partner with an icy stare. "That was very stupid, Garth."

"You're not a hunter!" Garth yelled. "You're a murderer! And I won't be part of this—"

With a *crack*, Strasser hit Garth squarely in the head with the butt of the rifle. "Anything else on your mind?" Strasser's question went unheard. Garth was bleeding and unconscious.

Strasser drew a semi-automatic pistol from his pocket. Using his gloved hand, he screwed on a barrel extension. There were more ways than one for a hunter to stalk his prey.

With purpose, with single-minded intent, Strasser moved through the crowd at the park. In the havoc, no one noticed the gun he held ready at his side.

Chapter 20

Just after the klieg light had shattered, Jill raised herself up on her elbows. "What was that?" she asked Gregg.

He had spotted the sparks, the flames, and the fire by the Ferris wheel. "Go find Joe," Gregg told her. "I'm gonna see if I can help over there." He ran toward the Ferris wheel.

Two new operators had taken over. They were unloading the ride as fast as they could amid fire and smoke and chaos. Parents pressed against the guardrail, snatched up their children, and held them tightly and close.

Gregg vaulted the rail and began to unload passengers directly from the moving buckets. The flames were growing stronger and the fire was out of control. At the base of the Ferris wheel, the engine exploded. The operator with the extinguisher was blown through the air, and the whole ride jerked to a halt.

There were only a couple of children to go. Two

little girls gripped the safety bar as their bucket swung back and forth. They were sobbing. "Mom! Mommy! Mommy!"

"Oh, my God!" their mother shouted. "Help! Somebody help!"

Gregg jumped atop the railing and leaped for the lurching bucket. The little girls were screaming and everything was violently shaking.

"Shhhh! Don't be scared," Gregg told them. "Climb down on my back." The two were nervous, unmoving and paralyzed. "Come on," Gregg urged. "Come on. Come on."

Tentatively, the two girls left the bucket, clutching onto Gregg's hair, his shoulders, and his back. They used him as a ladder and shimmied down his legs. One by one they dropped into the waiting arms of their mother.

Gregg let go, fell a good fifteen feet, landed roughly and rolled. The girls' mother was crying. "Thank you. Oh, thank you."

Winded, Gregg just nodded.

Jill moved through the maze of carnival games and finally spotted Joe. The small booths and bright buildings disoriented him. She called out to him, "Joe! Joe! Come, Joe!" But he didn't turn, didn't hear her.

And then there was Strasser, a couple of yards

from Jill, his gun leveled point-blank. He smiled at her startled expression of fear. But when her face changed, Strasser's smile faded. Instinctively, he sensed that Joe was behind him.

The gorilla hoisted the man into the air and roared deafeningly. The gun Strasser held went off, but the bullet aimed at nothing, hitting nothing. Joe howled again and crushed Strasser's left hand in his paw.

With a mighty force, Joe hurled his enemy into space. Strasser crashed through a booth and continued to fly until *whack*! He hung up on a power line.

Strasser caught desperately at the line with his gloved hand. He dangled there, safe for the moment, but directly below he could see the spark and crackle of electricity that came from several junction boxes blistered and maddened by the fire.

The glove began to slip off, his hold giving way. Strasser reached up with his good hand, but Joe's crushing grip had rendered it useless. Helplessly, hopelessly, Strasser plummeted down toward the junction boxes.

The boxes exploded in a shower of sparks. Above him, swinging, the black glove clung to the line.

Jill stood frozen. There were other witnesses, too, people who had seen Joe's violent actions, who had seen the gorilla throw Strasser to his fate. Among them was a swarm of police, led by Commander Gorman. "Get the marksmen up here!" Gorman ordered. "Now!"

Calling to Joe, Jill fled toward the Ferris wheel. She needed help. She had to find Gregg, and Jill knew that she alone wouldn't be able to convince the men to hold their fire. "Come, Joe! Run! *RUN!*"

Gregg was still there, catching his breath, when Jill threw herself into his arms. "Joe got Strasser. Strasser was trying to kill me."

"I know," Gregg said. "I understand. I just hope *they* do." He motioned toward the police officers that had surrounded them, rifles and marksmen ready.

Joe wasn't looking at the policemen. His gaze was directed at the Ferris wheel, burning steadily, the supports giving way, moorings loosening. At the very top of the wheel, Joe could see a bucket swinging, and two small hands holding on for dear life.

"Joe?" Jill said. "Joe? Come back!" The gorilla was running away from her, racing toward the Ferris wheel.

A sharpshooter followed the gorilla through the scope of his rifle. "Talk about an easy shot," he bragged. He had Joe right in the crosshairs when two people jumped in front of his gun.

"Stop!" Gregg was yelling. "Don't shoot him!"

Commander Gorman came forward, shouting at the intruders. "Get out of the way! Get back! Ready—aim—"

"Stop!" Jill shouted. "He's not dangerous! Please!"

"Get these people out of here," Gorman was barking orders. Several policemen were reaching for Jill and Gregg when there came another interruption. It was Jason's mother.

"Officer, help! Help me!" she pleaded. "I can't find my son. I think he's still on the Ferris wheel!"

"Look! Look!" Jill was waving her arms. Everyone turned to see Joe climbing the wheel, quickly, toward the endangered boy. And they could see the child's face up there, tiny, alone, and trapped.

Jason's mother was in agony. "Oh, God! Oh, Jason! Oh, help him, please!"

Jill faced her. "He'll save your boy," she said. "If they'll let him."

Jason's mother swallowed hard. "Don't shoot him," she begged Gorman. "Let him try. Please?"

Gorman raised his hands in the air. "Hold your fire. Hold your fire!"

Chapter 21

As Joe scaled the wheel, Jason gazed at the gorilla in wonderment. Joe lifted him from his seat. He pressed the boy safely against his chest, but there came a cracking, a tremor, and the whole Ferris wheel began to tilt.

By that time the amusement park was full of media, newscasters, and camera crews filming the rescue scene. Another explosion made the Ferris wheel shudder, and then tip to one side. "Oh, please, no!" Jason's mother screamed.

"It's going over!" Gregg yelled. "Get out of the way! Everybody!"

Slowly the wheel came apart, scattering flames and debris. And, as the wheel fell, Joe jumped. He hit the ground tremendously hard, the boy cradled in his arms.

The crowd was strangely silent amid the pop and crackle of fire. The gorilla was motionless. Only two figures were moving. Jill was running toward Joe, followed by Jason's mother.

Protected by the massive bulk of the gorilla, Jason looked up. "Mom?" he queried. "Mom?" Bursting into joyous tears, Jason's mother took him and folded her son into her arms.

Jill was crying, too. She knelt by Joe, stroking his great chest. The gorilla did not respond.

Gregg checked for a pulse, for a heartbeat, and for wounds, but Joe didn't stir. Jason's mother approached them. "I'm so sorry," she choked out. She recognized the grief of loss in Jill, the stab of a mother's sorrow.

Jill was beyond comfort. Softly, she hummed a lullaby, her mother's song.

She rested her cheek on Joe's giant hand. And then a huge finger twitched and gently touched Jill's face. It wasn't her imagination. Joe was alive. She kissed him frantically.

"That's right, Joe. That's right, big guy. That was a terrible fall, but you're okay, aren't you?" Jill was babbling in relief. "You're tough. You're so tough. Yes, you are. Yes, you are."

Gregg took a deep breath and let it out. "We've got to get him checked out," he said. "And get him somewhere safe."

"*Somewhere safe?*" Jill's voice was bitter. "Where would that be?"

Jason's mother broke in timidly, "Perhaps . . . I mean . . . maybe . . . isn't there something we can do?"

Jill shook her head. "No, I don't think so. Not unless you have a few million dollars to buy him a home somewhere."

Jason's mother nodded sadly. But Jason had also heard Jill's words. He pushed in front of his mother and pulled a crumpled dollar bill from his pocket. "Here," he offered. "For Joe."

The boy's eyes were shining with hope, and Gregg respectfully accepted the donation. "Thanks," he said. And then Gorman came forward, and several other policemen, all taking bills from their wallets.

Others followed suit. From the media, from the crowd, from all the people around, Gregg's pockets were being stuffed with money. "Here," they said. "Here. For Joe."

Across the nation, from coast to coast, people made contributions in the name of Joe Young. In New York City, busy commuters paused long enough to throw change into a bucket manned by a guy in a gorilla suit. And back in school, Jason collected pennies and nickels and bills.

In Africa, the villagers gave Kweli whatever could be spared. When a hand tapped him on the back, Kweli turned to see Pindi. "Here," Pindi said. "This is for Mighty Joe, bro."

And at the California Animal Conservancy, bags

of mail were delivered and received. Bags and bags of letters and cards, money and checks, many bearing foreign stamps, one addressed simply to: "Joe Young, America."

Epilogue

It had been some time since those at the conservancy had heard from Jill or Gregg. "Who'd have thought O'Hara would stay in one place for a month, much less a year," Harry marveled to Cecily. "He must be working some angle."

Cecily put a videotape into the VCR. "Shhh," she said. "Just watch."

The video showed a lush panorama of jungle and mountains and white floating clouds. It jiggled a little and panned over to Jill. "Sorry we've been out of touch for so long," she said. "But we've been really busy. We formally dedicated the park last week."

She pointed to a small sign and read the writing aloud: *"The Joe Young Wildlife Park: Dedicated to the belief that the world is big enough for all creatures to live in peace."*

There was a pause and Gregg stepped into the frame with Jill. He put his arm around her. "Hey! How's it going there, guys?"

Cecily glanced at Harry. "There's your angle."

They watched as Jill waved to someone or something off-screen. Gregg whistled, and the big form of Joe lumbered into the picture. Joe gave Gregg a delicate little gorilla kiss.

Then Gregg gave Jill a gorilla kiss. Cecily couldn't help but be touched. Her eyes misted, and maybe Harry's did, too.

Joe looked quizzically into the camera and pressed his giant face to the lens. Though everything went dark, the viewers knew that Joe had just sent them a kiss, long-distance from home.